The Bedraggled Dragon

Written by Diane Purdy
Illustrated by Eric Sawler

Make Magic!
Diane Purdy
2012

ISBN

978-1-77097-453-1 (Paperback)

978-1-77097-454-8 (eBook)

Library and Archives Canada Cataloguing in Publication

Purdy, Diane, 1933-

The bedraggled dragon / Diane Purdy ; illustrated by Eric Sawler.

Also issued in electronic format.

ISBN 978-1-77097-453-1

I. Sawler, Eric, 1985- II. Title.

PZ7.P98Be 2012   j813'.6   C2012-901816-3

Library and Archives Canada Cataloguing in Publication

Purdy, Diane, 1933-

The bedraggled dragon [electronic resource] / Diane

Purdy ; illustrated by Eric Sawler.

Electronic monograph issued in PDF format.

Also issued in print format.

ISBN 978-1-77097-454-8

I. Sawler, Eric, 1985- II. Title.

PZ7.P98Be 2012   j813'.6   C2012-901817-1

Published by:

FriesenPress

Suite 300 – 852 Fort Street

Victoria, BC, Canada V8W 1H8

www.friesenpress.com

Distributed to the trade by The Ingram Book Company

The Bedraggled Dragon
is dedicated to my loyal supporter,
sister Marcia Ganzel Roussos,
whom I love deeply.

Once upon a time...

...in Blissful Kingdom, there lived a dragon by the name of Darook, who was so handsome, with his shiny deep green scales and amazingly full sweeping tail that people came from far and wide to view this dragon to end all dragons.

"How very pleasing it is to have a mascot who brings us such fame," bragged all who lived in Blissful.

Thus every day was delightful.

The princesses loved going for romps through the meadows on Darook's broad back.

The princes spent happy hours hiding high amongst the tree leaves excitedly listening for his rip-snorting roar.

Until...that not-so-delightful day when Darook's best friend, Tessa the Tigress, rushed out of Faerie Forest very upset.

"Is it our imagination or are you very upset, Tessa?" questioned a Prince and Princess who'd been out and about searching for Darook, in vain.

"No, it's not your imagination," sobbed Tessa, "I am very upset about Darook!"

"Good heavens, why?" asked the Prince.

"Remember when Frunehilda the Faerie made us promise to stay away from Nasty Gnome's cave beneath the Rapid Waterfall?" reminded Tessa.

"Oh no, Nasty Gnome harmed Darook," sobbed the Princess.

"Darook is now bedraggled," said Tessa.

"Bedraggled?" questioned the Prince and Princess.

"Bedraggled," repeated Tessa.

"Last week, Darook begged me to sneak off with him to Rapid Waterfall to munch on berries," cried the tigress. "I wouldn't break my promise, but I should have told Frunehilda about his poor decision."

The children panicked, "We must inform the King and Queen."

As the children headed home, Orange Blossom, a Flower Maiden from Mountain Kingdom, skipped into the glen to find the dragon to end all dragons.

Her mascot, Flitterflutter, excitedly flew overhead. "I can't wait to see Darook."

At that exact moment, a dragon staggered out of Faerie Forest, munching on some dusky berries.

"Hello, lovely one," croaked the dragon. "Want to taste my berries?"

Flitterflutter swooped down, hovering over Darook, "My Flower Maiden is not allowed to take food from strangers."

Darook frowned at the creature fluttering overhead, "I am not a stranger. I'm Darook the Dragon, famous far and wide."

"How ridiculous," snickered the maiden, "I came to peek at the dragon to end all dragons, not a creature as bedraggled as you."

The Flower Maiden turned her back on Darook and scurried off toward Blissful Kingdom.

Flitterflutter pecked at Darook's head, "You're a disgrace to dragonhood." Then he flew off after his mistress.

Darook watched them in shock. This was the first time in his life he'd ever been called disgraceful.

The unhappy dragon didn't know what to do, so he sat down on a tree stump and munched on his berries.

Tessa ran into the clearing, bounding over to her best friend.

"The King and Queen insist you throw those berries away before they do you anymore harm."

Darook stood and turned his back on Tessa, nearly tripping over his tail.

"Be careful," cautioned the tigress. "Don't trip over your droopy tail."

"How dare you say my full sweeping tail is droopy!" sputtered the angry dragon.

"My dear friend," cried Tessa, "can't you tell how weak you've become?"

"No, I cannot," roared Darook. "Nasty Gnome promised his berries would make me feel happy forevermore. Now I need to pick more berries because you are seriously spoiling my happiness."

And Darook staggered towards the Rapid Waterfall.

Frunehilda the Faerie suddenly appeared and stared at Darook, in shock. "Zounds, Darook, what have you done to yourself?"

Tessa whispered to the faerie, "He's been eating the berries he found beneath Rapid Waterfall."

"Tattletale!" roared Darook.

"Heavenly Moon and Stars," lectured Frunehilda, "you promised."

"I fibbed," said the dragon, lifting his chin in defiance. "Nasty Gnome told me you'd be jealous because his magical dust is stronger than yours."

"Oh dear, Darook, don't you understand? Nasty Gnome has been using his Dark Dust of Doom to get you addicted to his berries," explained Frunehilda.

"Liar, liar, spit out fire," shouted the dragon.

"Just where is your fire, smarty pants?" questioned the tigress.

Darook glared, "It's still inside me. But now it's only visible to my friends, not tattletales like you, Tessa."

"Please, peer into my Magical Mirror of Truth," begged Frunehilda, as a golden mirror suddenly appeared in her upraised hand.

"I don't want to," sulked Darook. "Fiddly foop, Frunehilda, I'm fine."

"Then, you have nothing to fear," smiled the faerie. "If I'm mistaken, I will never mention the berries again."

Darook sighed, in relief, "It's a deal."

Frunehilda held her mirror towards the dragon.

Darook peered into the golden mirror, expecting to see his handsome self. "Oh, no, my deep green scales are gone, my eyes are baggy. I am bedraggled."

And with that, Darook the Dragon stumbled off towards Faerie Forest, embarrassed beyond belief.

Tessa began to run after Darook, but Frunehilda froze the tigress in place with a wave of her magical fingers.

"Darook needs time to think," consoled the faerie, as she waved her fingers, freeing Tessa. "The Magic Mirror of Truth shall tell us what to do."

In a flash, the mirror sparkled and a deep voice burst from within.

The dragon to end all dragons is about to expire. Nasty Gnome's evil berries have put out his fire. The berries are poisoned with a potion so strong. Only hours do remain to remedy the wrong...the wrong...the wrong.

"Please, do something, Frunehilda," howled Tessa.

Fruhehilda held her fingers up to the heavens and her mirror vanished, replaced by the Light Dust of Goodness.

"Light Dust of Goodness, flow from my fingers, make the Gnome's potion no longer linger. Light Dust of Goodness, come from within, Darook needs your goodness transferred to him," sighed the faerie.

Bolts of lightning filled the sky as Frunehilda flew towards the Rapid Waterfall.

The children rushed over to Tessa, "The kingdom's in an uproar!" Tessa explained how Frunehilda is planning to help Darook.

"Are you actually saying Frunehilda can save Darook with her Light Dust of Goodness?" asked the maiden.

The Prince smiled, "Frunehilda is our magical faerie."

The maiden giggled in relief. "Meeting the three of you has been the only nice thing that's happened since I arrived...besides tasting the Queen's golden cupcakes.

"After what's happened, I believe we should all only eat healthy foods from now on," advised Tessa.

"The King is creating a Proclamation requiring everyone in the land to do just that," reassured the Prince.

Flitterflutter began wildly flying about in circles, looking towards Faerie Forest.

In a flash, Frunehilda the Faerie reappeared, searching this way and that.

Tessa questioned the faerie, "Is Darook back to his old self?"

"When I sprinkled him with the Light Dust of Goodness, he let out an earsplitting roar and ran deeper into Faerie Forest," answered Frunehilda.

The faerie reached up to the heavens and the mirror magically appeared in her hand. "Children, please help send our well wishes for Darook."

"Magical Mirror of Truth, pure as a golden bell, we love our dear dragon, please help make him well," all pleaded.

And with an earth shattering flash of lightening, the mirror bellowed out its reply.

Frunehilda the Faerie's Light Dust of Goodness has saved your dear dragon, but tell him he must never again eat berries from the Gnome. Light Dust helps only once so he is now on his own...own...own...

With a mighty roar, Darook bounded onto the meadow, his scales deep green, his tail full and swishy. "Guess whoooo?"

"It's the real you," howled Tessa, hugging her friend.

The Princess held Frunehilda's hand, "Please please, make sure Nasty Gnome never harms Darook again."

The Prince agreed, "Use your Light Dust of Goodness to destroy his berries and trap Nasty Gnome in his cave, forevermore."

"Yes, indeedy," chirped Flitterflutter.

"Oh my, this is not an easy decision," said Frunehilda. "I must consult the King."

"Our King will create another Proclamation if he wants to keep our dragon safe," insisted the Prince.

Orange Blossom was shocked, "I want Darook safe from Nasty Gnome, too. But, my King insists we all think for ourselves and never make excuses for our poor decisions."

The birdie chirped, "Yes, indeedy."

"Flitterflutter is a flipperflopper," laughed Frunehilda.

Darook whispered to the Flower Maiden, "Now do you believe I am who I am?"

"My mascot and I came to Blissful to see the dragon to end all dragons...and that most certainly is you," giggled Orange Blossom.

Darook spoke to Frunehilda, "Please, don't use your dust to save me from me."

The faerie kissed Darook's head. "Does that mean you won't ever again break your promises?"

"As Flitterflutter would say, 'yes indeedy.' One is only as trustworthy as one's word," lectured the dragon.

The Princess cheered, "Let us inform everyone that Blissful Kingdom is back to normal."

"Orange Blossom, come celebrate with us," smiled the Prince. "After sharing a healthy meal, Darook will fly you home on his back."

"My pleasure," bowed Darook. "and Flitterflutter may ride on my head."

Flitterflutter dropped down onto Darook's head, chirping happily.

Frunehilda smiled, "This is the perfect ending to a day that might have ended quite poorly."

Her laughter tinkled in the breeze as she disappeared from view.

Darook let out a happy roar, "And I promise, from this day forward, whenever I see junk food being eaten, I'll shoot flames from my nostrils and sizzle the junk food to a frazzle...except for the Queen's golden cupcakes, of course."

"Hooray for Darook the Dragon," cheered Orange Blossom and Flitterflutter.

"Hooray for Darook the Dragon," cheered the Prince and Princess.

"Hooray for Darook the Dragon," cheered Tessa the Tigress.

"Aw shucks," blushed Darook the Dragon, "I love you all."

And every day in Blissful Kingdom became delightful once again.

After all, what other Kingdom could boast a mascot like Darook...the dragon to end all dragons?

And everyone lived happily ever after!

CPSIA information can be obtained
at www.ICGtesting.com
Printed in the USA
LVIW010012210612
286729LV00002B